To

Jason

From

Sarah

Date

Christmas
1999

I love you
very much!

Caleb

Caleb
A Very Shy Angel

Stories by Joanne De Jonge
Illustrations by Samuel J. Butcher

Baker Books
A Division of Baker Book House Co
Grand Rapids, Michigan 49516

Precious Moments art © 1979, 1981, 1987, 1996
by Precious Moments, Inc.

Text © 1997 by Joanne De Jonge

Published by Baker Books
a division of Baker Book House Company
P.O. Box 6287, Grand Rapids, MI 49516-6287

Printed in the United States of America

Library of Congress Cataloging-in-Publication Data

De Jonge, Joanne E., 1943–
  Precious moments Caleb : a very shy angel / Joanne De Jonge.
     p.   cm.
    Summary: Caleb, the newest angel in heaven, finds that he has a lot to
learn, but he is fortunate to get a little extra help from Jesus.
    ISBN 0-8010-4295-X
    [1. Angels—Fiction. 2. Christian life—Fiction.] I. Title.
PZ7.D3678Pr   1997
[Fic]—dc21   97-24113

For current information about all releases from Baker Book House, visit our web site:
http://www.bakerbooks.com

Contents

Preface to Parents

In Sophie you met a lovable, sometimes rambunctious angel, who, as the newest angel in heaven, had a lot to learn about angelic behavior. Now, get ready to follow the escapades of Caleb, who has taken Sophie's place as the newest angel in heaven.

Watch as Caleb learns to rely on his angel friends for answers to his many questions and encouragement to face new experiences. He's a shy angel who wonders about his purpose and place in heaven among the other angels, but he learns to be bold in completing the tasks given him by Jesus. Caleb's curiosity and gentle spirit will touch you as you follow his story.

As you read these stories with your children, help them identify with Caleb as he searches for his special place in heaven and let them share in his relief when he finds rest in the arms of Jesus. Teach them to delight in the way even a shy angel can make a difference to those around him by using the special gifts God has given to him.

Let your children take lessons from Caleb's adventures and apply them to their own lives. Allow them to mirror his discoveries about special God-given gifts and purpose in life. But most of all, remind them of their precious place in your heart.

Caleb's Gift

Caleb sat in a field at the edge of heaven, lost in thought. He wanted to give Jesus a gift, but he didn't know what that gift should be.

You see, Caleb was heaven's newest angel, and he had much to learn. He had lots of love—all heavenly angels do—but he didn't have much experience yet. And he knew nothing at all about giving gifts to Jesus.

"After I've learned more about the heavenly ways, I'll know exactly what to do," he sighed to himself. "But I want to show Jesus that I love him now. What can I give him?" he wondered as he sat in his favorite heavenly place.

It's a little-known fact that most angels have a favorite place in heaven. Caleb loved his heavenly mansion. He also loved the streets of gold, and he would

often stare in wonder at the pearly gates. He liked to sit on a cloud and watch mortals on earth. (Angels always call people who live on earth mortals.) Better yet, he loved to sit by the river of life and dangle his feet in its crystal waters. But most of all, he loved heaven's wonderful fields, because flowers grew there.

12

Heaven's flowers are, of course, more beautiful than anything ever seen on earth. Mortals can't imagine their brilliant colors or their heavenly perfumes. They haven't seen such a wide variety of flowers either. Countless kinds of flowers paint heaven's fields. And each perfect flower lives forever.

Caleb sighed and buried his chubby little face in a flower. "Any gift that I give Jesus will probably be wrong," he thought. "And all the other angels will see it and laugh. With love, of course," he quickly added. "But they'll all look at me. Besides that, Jesus doesn't need my gifts. Yet I want to show him my love. I wish I dared ask Sophie about this."

Sophie had been the newest angel in heaven for a very long time. So, shortly after Caleb appeared, the two of them had become the best of friends. Sophie had shown Caleb around heaven and

even introduced him to Jesus. Now she was helping him to learn the heavenly ways and meet all the heavenly hosts. Because Caleb was rather shy, he took his time to meet the other angels. But Sophie wasn't one bit shy, so the two fit together well.

"Did I hear my name?" Sophie asked as she landed gently next to him. "I figured that you were out here. I know you've got a question, and we'll talk about it soon. But first, I've got a surprise for you!

"I must visit earth right away. I'm a guardian angel, as you know, and my mortal—a little boy in Israel—needs some help. Anyway, I'm supposed to take you with me! It's time for you to learn more about mortals."

With that she took Caleb's hand, walked to the far end of the field, and jumped off the edge. "Make yourself invisible and don't say or do anything," she warned as they got closer to the earth. "You may only whisper to me. Otherwise, just watch."

Silently the two angels landed beside Sophie's charge. He sat in a courtyard, shivering. A winter wind blasted Israel, and the young lad was very, very cold.

"He has no coat," Sophie whispered. "He'll get sick unless I do something about it quickly. But I may not simply give him a coat. My orders are to use another mortal. I must find Dorcas."

"Who is Dorcas?" Caleb whispered as quietly as he could.

"She's a very kind woman who lives nearby. She's always making clothes for other people. Maybe she has an extra coat. There she is."

Caleb watched as the gate to the courtyard opened and a woman walked in. Sophie flew right over to the woman and whispered something to her. The woman looked at the small boy and left.

"I've just put a thought into her heart," Sophie whispered to Caleb. "We'll see if it works."

Sure enough. A few minutes later Dorcas returned to the courtyard. This time she carried a small coat.

"David, sweetheart," she called. "I made this woolen coat for my nephew. But he doesn't need it. Let's see if it fits you." She helped the little boy put on the coat. Of course, it fit perfectly.

"You'll take it, won't you, David?" Dorcas asked sweetly. "My house is too small for all the extra clothes I make. Wear it with love, sweetheart, and God go with you," she added. Then she left the courtyard and went back to her home.

"Done," Sophie whispered. "Let's go." She took Caleb's hand again and they flew toward heaven.

"Let's rest here," Sophie suggested as they neared a large fluffy cloud. "Do you have any questions about anything that happened down there?"

"What's a sweetheart?" Caleb asked.

"Oh, that's what mortals sometimes call each other. They think that love comes from their hearts. So sometimes they draw hearts to picture love. Or they give heart-shaped things to mortals they love. Anyway, they often call each other 'sweetheart.'"

"And what did Dorcas mean when she said, 'God go with you'?" Caleb asked.

"That was her way of wishing God's love and blessing on David," Sophie explained. "You see, Dorcas loves Jesus very much, and she shows that love by helping people. Jesus told mortals that whatever they do for each other, they do for him. Her gift to David was really a gift to Jesus."

Caleb thought for a moment. "You mean," he asked slowly, "that if I give

18

something to a mortal, it's like I am giving it to Jesus?"

"I never thought about that," Sophie answered him. "Jesus was talking to mortals, not angels, when he said that. Besides, we can't do whatever we want for mortals. We don't know God's plan for them. So we wait for God to tell us what to do. Now, Caleb, what was that question you had before we left?"

"Oh, nothing really. I just have to think for a while. Thanks, Sophie." And Caleb flew back to his favorite field. He was just a bit too timid to ask Sophie all his questions. Besides that, he had an idea.

"I'll give Jesus my heart!" His thoughts tumbled over each other in excitement. "I can't take my real heart out and hand it to Jesus. So I'll make a perfect little heart. Because I made it, it will be *my* heart. I'll give *that* to Jesus! Sophie said that humans give heart-shaped things to mortals they love. That's what I'll give Jesus! He'll understand."

Immediately Caleb set to work to make his gift. First, he found the purest red flowers that grew in heaven. Then, as a test, he gently picked one petal from a flower. Immediately a soft new petal appeared on the flower to make it perfect again. Then he picked a petal from another flower, and another, and another. Each grew a new perfect petal.

Caleb almost burst with joy as he flew back to his mansion and fetched a golden bowl. "I'll make the perfect heart," he sang to himself as he filled the bowl with perfect red petals. "That will be my gift to Jesus." And he sat down among the flowers to fashion his heart.

One by one Caleb took petals from the bowl and pressed them together. Every time he picked up a new petal, he blew on it gently. His breath added an extra bit of love to each petal. And it moistened each petal, so that the petals clung together to form a red lump. Then, carefully, he rolled that red lump between his chubby little hands to give it shape.

"It's a perfect heart for Jesus," he sang to himself. And he rolled and molded, pushed and prodded the heart. Caleb worked on this gift for a long, long time. Finally, he had just the shape he

wanted. He held it up and looked at it with shining eyes. "Perfect!"

Now, Caleb didn't know—and Sophie hadn't explained—that mortals draw heart shapes different from their real hearts. Caleb had never seen the heart shapes that mortals draw. But he had seen real mortal hearts. And so that's the shape he made. Caleb's "perfect" heart looked exactly like a real heart.

"What's that, Caleb?" Sophie suddenly appeared beside him. Caleb quickly hid the heart behind his back. It was *too* personal to show Sophie.

"Oh, well," Sophie changed the subject. "Remember Dorcas? I just came to tell you that she's in some sort of trouble. She's very sick and could die. But God has said that it's not her time yet. All the heavenly hosts are watching to see what happens. You may want to watch too. This is a good way to learn about how angels do God's work on earth. Most of us are gathered on the cloud closest to earth. You're welcome to join us." And with that, she disappeared.

A thought struck Caleb. "This is the perfect time to see Jesus! Most other angels won't be nearby, so I won't have to do this in front of older, wiser angels. Even if I make a mistake, Jesus will understand." And he held his heart high to take one last look at it.

"Oh, no!" he gasped. "It's not perfect anymore. I must have bumped it when I put it behind my back."

Caleb was right. His flower-petal heart was missing a piece. A petal had fallen off and left a slight dent on one side of the heart. Caleb frantically searched for the missing petal. But he couldn't find it.

"I can't add another petal now," he thought desperately. "That will take too

long. Then all the angels will be back. I'll never dare to give this to Jesus in front of them. I must go now." So he took the heart in both hands and very carefully winged his way toward the heavenly city. He made sure he avoided the cloud on which the angels clustered, so that none would see him. Then he stopped and took a deep breath before he went to Jesus.

Ever so shyly, Caleb peeked around a corner. No other angel stood near Jesus. Then, with his head bowed, he stepped from behind the corner and walked on shaking legs to Jesus. He dropped to his knees. And, without daring to speak or look up, he offered the heart in his outstretched hands.

"It's perfect," Jesus said. And he gently took the heart from Caleb's small hands. "Precious Caleb," he continued as he bent down and gathered Caleb into his lap. "I've been waiting for you."

"Perfect? Waiting for me?" Caleb was puzzled, but he looked at Jesus happily. Love shone from Jesus' face and washed over the little angel.

"Stay right here with me, and you will understand," Jesus said in answer to Caleb's thoughts.

Suddenly, another angel flashed into Jesus' presence. "Dorcas is dead," the angel said, panting from the quick flight. "Your disciple Peter is trying to raise her, but he needs your strength."

"I've heard his prayers," Jesus answered. "Dorcas's heart sleeps. It's tired. This is what she needs." And he took the heart that Caleb had made and handed it to the angel.

"A heavenly heart?" the angel wondered. "No mortal has ever had a perfect heart from heaven."

"This is perfect for Dorcas," Jesus said. "It's full of love. Use it."

30

Caleb sat, speechless with love and with wonder. His gift to Jesus had become a gift to a mortal! Jesus had taken his imperfect gift and made it perfect! He sat, perfectly happy, on Jesus' lap for a very long time.

So long, in fact, that all the heavenly hosts returned and gathered around Jesus. Dorcas was alive again, and the angels praised God. And they smiled with love at heaven's newest angel, who had given Jesus the perfect gift.

That happened a long, long time ago. Since then, Caleb has learned much more about heaven and love and gifts. But he never did find that missing petal.

You see, the breeze from Sophie's wings had whisked the petal completely off

the heavenly field. As the two angels talked, that one perfect red petal had floated gently to earth. There it took root and grew as earth's first red rose.

And that's why roses are often used today as gifts of love. They're Caleb's special reminder to mortals: Gifts of love are gifts to Jesus.

Caleb's Problem

Caleb had a problem. Not a really big, terrible problem, as people sometimes have. Angels don't have problems like that, and Caleb was an angel. But he did have a little question deep in his heart. (That's as close as angels ever come to having problems.) You see, Caleb wondered if he really belonged in heaven.

Oh, he loved Jesus; there wasn't any question about that. He had even given Jesus his heart, but that's another story. That had been a long time ago, when Caleb was a very new angel. Since then, he had watched and listened and learned more about heaven's ways. And now he wondered, once in a while, if he really belonged.

That's what he was thinking about as he sat on a curb of a golden street. He watched all the other angels come and go about their business.

"They all look like they know for sure that they belong in heaven," he noticed. "Stephanie's probably taking a message to another angel. She knows all of the heavenly hosts." He watched the very mature angel brush right past him toward a heavenly mansion.

"The heavenly choir must be ready to practice," Caleb thought aloud. An uncountable number of angels flittered gracefully overhead. He ducked to miss the bottom of a harp carried by a rather careless angel.

Then Sophie swooped past him with a grin and a wave. "She's probably going to help the mortal she guards," he said a little louder. (Angels always call people who live on earth mortals.)

"Hey, they're all doing something," he realized suddenly and said loudly. He snapped his chubby little fingers with an idea. "I've got it now! I have to *do* something! Then I'll really belong." With that he flew back to his mansion to think some more.

But very soon Caleb was back on the golden streets, walking with purpose toward the pearly gates. "I'll make myself heaven's gatekeeper," he said with a grin.

And so for a while Caleb worked as a gatekeeper to heaven. Every time a mortal soul came to the pearly gates, Caleb greeted it and ushered it into heaven. But he knew that he was inventing work for himself. You see, heaven's gates are always open.

So he tried cleaning up after all the heavenly feasts. But angels are very neat creatures who always leave their plates perfectly clean. And they never, ever spill anything on the floor of the great banquet hall. So there wasn't anything to clean up.

Caleb even considered joining the heavenly choir. But he was a shy angel, and he didn't really trust his voice. What if he became all choked up? What if he couldn't hit the high notes? "The other angels probably sing so much better than I do," he thought to himself.

Rather dejected and feeling quite out of place, Caleb flew to one of his favorite clouds to watch the world go by. He always felt just a little bit better when he saw how mortals bumbled around down on earth.

With a rustle of wings and a soft breeze Sophie suddenly landed next to him. Sophie was his very best angel friend.

"Precious Caleb," she said sweetly, "what is wrong? You look like you're not completely happy." And she folded one soft wing around the sweet little cherub.

Caleb gulped twice to swallow his words. He just couldn't bring himself to talk about it. But Sophie knew. Angels know each other perfectly. "Oh, Caleb," she sighed. "You wonder if you really belong here, don't you?" Caleb sniffed and nodded.

"Of course you belong, because God made you and put you here. God doesn't make mistakes. And we all know how much you love Jesus.

"You've been very sweet lately," she continued. "I know that you've welcomed mortals to heaven. And you've tried to clean up after feasts. It almost seems like you're trying to work your way into heaven. Don't you know, Caleb, that you can't earn heaven? God put you here. You don't have to work for it.

"Do you know what I think?" Sophie continued with a grin. "I think that you're watching earth too much. You're almost starting to think like a mortal.

"Some of them don't understand God's plan. They try to work their way into heaven. But they can't because it's a gift for them and for us."

Sophie sighed heavily as she went on. "And they're always breaking off into snobby little groups. The rich look down on the poor. Adults shut out kids. And Jews won't be seen with Gentiles. Satan is working hard down there on earth. It's a problem, believe me. I run into it all the time when I'm on guardian duty. But enough of that. I've come to give you an assignment from God."

Caleb sat up straight. He had a job to do for God! Maybe he really did belong. He almost jumped off his cloud with joy. "What, Sophie, what?" he bubbled. "What do I get to do?"

"Calm down, Caleb," she said serenely. "You're to bring a message to earth—"

"Oh, no! I hope I don't have to sing it," he interrupted.

"Of course not," Sophie chuckled. "God knows how you feel about singing. But he's heard you speak to newly arrived souls. You're very good at making them feel comfortable. That's why God is sending you.

"You're to speak to a Gentile named Cornelius. That's all I know. God wants you to be ready to go any time. He'll make sure that you know the message by the time you need it. For now, just be sure you can say the name Cornelius." And with that, Sophie disappeared.

"Cornelius." Caleb said the name slowly. "Cornelius, Cornelius, Cornelius." That was good; he had the name down pat. But, just in case, he practiced as he ambled back to his mansion. "Cornelius, Cornelius, Cornelius . . ."

Several times, Caleb perched on clouds far at heaven's edge to watch mortals on earth. Sometimes he even listened in on their conversations.

"Who is Cornelius?" he often wondered. "What's he like?" Soon, Caleb knew every single Cornelius who lived on earth. And he watched them all. For hours on end, he'd peer over the side of his cloud, watching a Cornelius.

So Sophie knew exactly where to find the little angel the next time she went looking for him. She landed so quietly, and he was concentrating so hard, that he didn't hear her.

"Caleb," she whispered. Then a bit louder, "Caleb! Caleb! Come quickly!" She tugged on his robe. "It's time to give your message to Cornelius! Not *that* Cornelius," she added when she saw the mortal Caleb had been watching. "The Cornelius you'll visit is a Gentile living in Caesarea. See him? He's on his knees, praying."

Caleb looked where she pointed. "OK. I know him too. What should I say?"

"God will give you the words as you speak," Sophie answered. "But you must remember that this Cornelius is a Gentile. Not many Gentiles have seen angels, so you will need to speak very clearly.

"Cornelius belongs to God, but *he's* not entirely sure that he does. Caleb, you know how *that* feels. Be very loving and gentle with him. And remember, speak only the words that God gives you to speak."

"Cornelius," Caleb said one last time as he jumped lightly from the cloud. He felt the heat of summer as he approached Caesarea. And he could see Cornelius sweat uncomfortably in the heat.

"Be gentle," Sophie had said. So, while he was still invisible, Caleb slowly waved his wings over the praying man. That stirred up a soft breeze that cooled the mortal's warm cheeks and lifted his hair ever so slightly. Caleb could hear Cornelius sigh in response.

Then he made himself visible and stood before the kneeling Gentile. "Cornelius," he said, softly, but very clearly.

"What is it, Lord?" Cornelius answered. He looked straight at Caleb.

Caleb opened his mouth, and the Lord spoke through him. "Your prayers and gifts to the poor have come up as a remembrance before God," he said. "Now send men to Joppa to bring back a man named Simon who is called Peter. He is staying with Simon the tanner, whose house is by the sea."

Caleb gasped. He was so surprised by what he had said that he almost forgot to make himself invisible again.

"What's going on?" he thought in a rush. "Cornelius is a Gentile and Peter is a Jew. This Gentile will ask a Jew to visit him—on *my* orders! This is just asking for trouble! Did I make a mistake? I'd better watch."

And so Caleb watched the scene unfold. Just as he had ordered, Cornelius sent someone to get Peter. A few days later, Peter showed up at Cornelius's house. The first words from Peter's  mouth almost brought Caleb to tears: "You are well aware that it is against our law for a Jew to associate with a Gentile or visit him."

"Oh, no!" Caleb shook his head slowly. "Now Peter will probably tell Cornelius that Gentiles don't belong to God. I can't watch." He shot up to a low-flying cloud.

"Now what?" he wondered. "I must have made a mistake in the message. I for sure don't belong in heaven. I don't care what Sophie said." And Caleb fell into a very blue mood. He sat on that cloud, almost crying, for hours.

"Precious Caleb, I've heard so much about you. It's time we met." The voice was deep and strong, and very reassuring.

Caleb looked up and saw the most magnificent angel he had ever met. The stranger was very tall, with broad shoulders and huge white wings. He wore his halo very straight and carried a trumpet under one arm. Love shone from his eyes, and his deep voice was kindness itself.

"I'm Gabriel, God's chief messenger angel," he said. "I've been sent to tell you that you did *not* make a mistake. God is very pleased with the way you delivered that message. Now, come back to heaven with me. I have something to show you."

When they were seated in Caleb's favorite field, Gabriel continued. "I've been thinking that maybe you would like this." From his sleeve he took a small golden trumpet.

"For me?" Caleb asked in wonder. "This is *my* trumpet? You want me to play this trumpet?"

"Of course," Gabriel replied. "This trumpet will be your voice of praise. I'll give you lessons, of course."

Right then and there, Gabriel gave Caleb his very first trumpet lesson.

Yes, Caleb learned to play the trumpet as easily as many angels learn to play harps. He was naturally good at it. Soon Caleb could play every praise tune, summons tune, and melody ever heard in heaven. He loved to stand in a field among the flowers and practice his trumpet.

And so it happened some time later that Sophie found Caleb in a flower-dotted field, practicing his trumpet.

"Caleb, come quickly," she called to him breathlessly. "A new soul will enter heaven soon. The choir will sing, and *you* must play the trumpet with them!"

Together the two angels quickly flew to the pearly gates. Sophie stepped into the choir, and Caleb took his place to one side. He glanced up and smiled as Gabriel landed next to him and softly put a hand on his shoulder. All was silent as the heavenly hosts waited for the new soul.

Then Caleb saw him slowly approaching the pearly gates. The choir burst into joyous song just as the little angel recognized the soul.

"Cornelius!" he gasped aloud. "That's my Cornelius! I didn't think he belonged."

"Oh, but he does," Gabriel leaned down and spoke in Caleb's ear. "Cornelius loves Jesus. And everyone who loves Jesus belongs!"

In a flash, Caleb understood. Anyone who loves Jesus belongs! Of course, Caleb had always belonged. He had always loved Jesus. Sophie had told him that, but he didn't dare believe it. Now he saw proof from God before his very eyes. Cornelius belonged, and so did Caleb!

That day, Caleb played the most joyous welcome song ever heard in heaven. The notes soared and the melody sang, and all the heavenly hosts heard it and rejoiced.

Caleb has played many times now to welcome souls to heaven. And he's especially good when a shy soul, or one who has felt left out, comes home. Then his songs of welcome echo with special joy throughout the heavens.

In fact, Caleb is even good with mortals who wonder if they belong. When the days are especially hot and there's no whisper of wind on earth,

Caleb visits such mortals. They may feel a soft breeze cool their cheeks and lift their hair ever so slightly. That's Caleb's way of saying, "Anyone who loves Jesus belongs to him."

Caleb's Prayer

Caleb knelt in a corner of his heavenly mansion and prayed.

Angels do pray, you know. Most of the time their prayers are all praise to God. Or they're prayers of love that just tumble from angels' lips. But once in a while they include a little request to God. Angels pray from wherever they happen to be at the time.

Caleb happened to be in his mansion. He had been gathering his glitter dust, lost in thought. He couldn't imagine being any happier than he was. But he *could* imagine having a full-time job as one of the heavenly hosts. He had been heaven's newest angel for quite some time now, free to roam where he pleased and do what he pleased. Once in a while he had a special assignment, and he loved doing whatever God wanted

him to do. But now he thought that he was ready for a full-time position. So he knelt there in a corner full of glitter dust and told God he felt ready for full-time work.

But nothing happened right away. Jesus didn't walk in and tell him what job was his. Nothing changed.

So Caleb put the glitter dust into his golden bowls and delivered them to Sophie's mansion. Sophie was in charge of sending the glitter dust to earth as shimmering snow.

"Maybe I could ask to guard some mortal," he thought lazily as he sat down in a field of golden flowers. (Angels always call people who live on earth mortals.) "I love to watch them on earth."

But he quickly dismissed that idea. "Satan's always busy down there," he thought. "I can handle that for a while. But I think God uses very bold angels for full-time guardian duty. I'm not very bold." He bent to smell a flower. "Aachoo," he sneezed as a petal tickled his nose.

"God bless you," said a familiar voice above him. Sophie gently landed next to him.

"God always blesses me, Sophie," Caleb answered. "But he isn't blessing me with an answer right now."

"Oh, the full-time job bit," Sophie said, reading his thoughts. "You know that God has an answer. Be patient, Caleb. When the time is just right, God will answer you. By the way, thanks for the glitter dust."

"But what do you think my job will be?" the little angel asked impatiently.

"You are very good with messages, Caleb," said a new voice.

"Stephanie," Caleb greeted her brightly. "Please sit right here between us."

Stephanie had been in heaven since the beginning of time and knew every angel there. She often delivered messages to other angels and kept them all up to date on heaven's activities.

"I've got a message for you, Caleb." Stephanie smiled at the eager little angel. "No, it's not about your full-time job yet. God wants you to go to Israel to help Peter. He's in jail right now."

Caleb raised his eyebrows and a little crease appeared on his forehead.

"I know," the angel continued serenely. "You've never freed someone from prison. But you did watch Marcus go to free the disciples and God will give you strength.

"You are so good at comforting mortals, that God wants you to go this time. Peter's friends have been praying. It's time for an answer."

"You mean, *I'm* to answer some prayers?" Caleb asked, astonished at the thought. "I thought that God answered prayers."

"Of course he does," Sophie answered. "But sometimes he uses angels, and sometimes he even uses mortals."

"How can mortals answer prayer?" Caleb wondered aloud.

"You may find out soon," Stephanie answered quietly. "When mortals act in love, they're almost as good as angels. Anyway, you'd better take care of your assignment. Come, Sophie, let's go." Both angels quickly disappeared with a poof.

Caleb flew as fast as he could to a large cloud that shadowed the earth. Gripping the sides tightly, he leaned over and looked down.

Many laser-like beams of light bridged the gap between earth and heaven. But several beams came from one spot on earth. "No doubt about it," Caleb thought when he saw the beams. "That's where the prayers are coming from."

It's a little-known fact that angels can see mortal prayers. Every prayer is like a little beam of energy shot toward heaven. When angels concentrate, they can see these beams. Of course, angels don't see prayer beams all the time. That would confuse them. But when they must, they can see any prayer beam they choose.

Caleb sat for just a moment, looking at the prayer beams.

"I'll just follow that cluster down to the right place," he thought. "It looks like they're coming from Israel." And he stood up, jumped off the cloud, and winged his way to earth.

Now, Caleb had never followed a prayer beam before this. He knew it could be done, but this was his very first try. And he became just a little confused. He zeroed in on the wrong prayer beams. They were not from Peter's friends but from believers on other parts of the earth. That threw him off course.

He was almost to earth before he realized that the country below did not look at all like Israel. So, quickly he detoured to the moon to rest and get his bearings.

"My goodness, it's cold here," Caleb thought. "Oh, dear, I've landed on the dark side of the moon." So, as fast as he could, he scampered over to the light side.

Not many angels walk on the moon, so its surface is very dusty. As he scampered across the moon, Caleb kicked up a lot of that dust. It sailed into the air and soon fell into orbit around the moon. Caleb thought nothing of it until he looked down to earth for his landing place.

It was almost midnight in Israel, but hundreds of Jews crowded Jerusalem's streets. They all stood staring at the moon. Caleb could hear the "oohs" and "aahs" as they wondered about that new moon glow.

"It's so beautiful," a child said.

"What is it?" asked a rabbi.

"Maybe it's a message from God," suggested a priest.

"Oh, dear," Caleb thought. "That's no message. I'd better get rid of it." Quickly, he blew the moon dust out into space. One by one, the people returned to their homes.

Once more Caleb zeroed in on the prayer beams, this time making certain that he had the right beams. Then he followed them very carefully, right to the heart of Jerusalem. Making sure he was invisible, he landed very near the prison.

"Mommy! Daddy! Where are you?" a tiny voice cried in the night. Caleb looked around quickly. A little boy sat slumped against the prison wall. Tears ran down his cheeks. Caleb understood immediately.

"He's lost. I sure know how that feels," he said to himself. "God, let me help him."

Somewhere down the street a gate slammed. An old man came outside to take one last look at the moon. In a flash, Caleb sped to the man's side. The man turned to go inside, but Caleb barred the way.

"I guess I'm just not ready to go in yet," the man said to himself. "Maybe I should take a

walk first . . ." Caleb quickly turned him toward the prison. "I guess I'll go this way," the man finished.

"Mommy! Daddy! I'm lost," wailed the child.

"What's this?" wondered the man. "Is this Moshe ben Zadok?" He stooped and lifted the little boy into his arms. "What are you doing out here?"

"Oh, Rabbi," the child sobbed, "I'm lost in the dark. Where's Mommy?"

Caleb followed the pair as the rabbi took the child's hand and led him home.

"Moshe, Moshe," his mother smothered him with kisses. "We were so worried. Thank you, Rabbi. You were an answer to prayer."

Caleb's ears perked up. So, that's the way it worked. God had used him to use a mortal to answer a prayer. But he had been sent in answer to other prayers. Without delay, he flew right through the prison walls to Peter's cell.

Peter was fast asleep, of course. He lay between two soldiers, bound to each by chains. Caleb studied the situation for a minute, then knew exactly what to do.

He made himself visible and very, very bright. His light filled the whole cell. Then he shook Peter, but Peter slept on. Finally he hit Peter lightly on the side.

"Peter, Peter," he called. Peter woke up and opened his eyes.

"Quick, get up!" Caleb said urgently. He touched the chains and they fell from Peter's wrists. "Put on your clothes and your sandals," Caleb urged. "Wrap your cloak around you and follow me." Caleb glanced at the soldiers and willed them to sleep on. Then, walking just like a human, he led Peter out of his cell.

At each locked gate Caleb hesitated slightly and concentrated very hard. Each gate trembled, then swung open. Caleb stared at the guards they passed, willing each to sleep. And each slept on, as if in a trance.

Finally, Caleb and Peter left the prison and stood in the street. Caleb concentrated on the prayer beams again. He couldn't miss the laser lights of many colors that came from a house two blocks away. He pointed Peter in the right direction, walked with him for one block, then disappeared.

Peter got the idea and walked straight to the house. Caleb stayed close by, yet invisible. He wanted to see Peter safe with his friends. He held his breath as Peter knocked on the outer gate. A young girl came to the gate.

"Rhoda!" Peter said. The girl turned around and ran back inside.

"Oh, no!" Caleb groaned. "Now what?" Immediately he flew into the house.

"Peter's here!" he heard Rhoda exclaim.

"You're out of your mind," Peter's friends answered. "It must be his angel."

"What do I do next?" Caleb thought desperately. "Don't you believe in prayer? Keep knocking, Peter. Don't quit," he almost said aloud.

Peter understood. He kept right on knocking until they let him in.

Only then did Caleb figure his job was done. Exhausted, he began a slow return to heaven. He even took a few minutes to rest once more on the moon. But this time he was very careful not to stir up any moon dust.

When Caleb reached heaven's gates, Jesus himself stood ready to meet him. Immediately, Caleb fell to his knees. But Jesus stooped down and gently lifted the trembling angel into his arms.

"Well done, my precious Caleb," he said softly. "Now it is time for your full-time job."

So Caleb heard straight from Jesus that he was to be heaven's very first angel-at-large. This meant that Caleb would help out with all kinds of different things and do whatever job Jesus needed him to do each day.

All of heaven celebrated with Caleb. The choir sang and Gabriel himself played the trumpet. All the angels danced in happiness, then enjoyed a heavenly feast. And Caleb, heaven's newest angel, became Caleb, heaven's first angel-at-large.

That all happened a very, very long time ago. Since then, Caleb has been an absolutely wonderful angel-at-large. He helps out wherever he can. Sometimes he delivers messages for Stephanie when she's very busy. Sometimes he

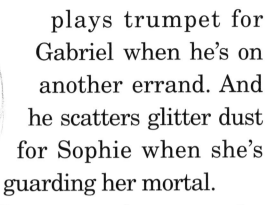

plays trumpet for Gabriel when he's on another errand. And he scatters glitter dust for Sophie when she's guarding her mortal.

But, most importantly, Caleb works with mortals. Sometimes he helps guard a mortal. Sometimes he brings a vision to one. But usually he helps answer mortal prayers. Once in a while he works directly. But most often he simply moves mortals to act in love. They rarely know that they're an answer to prayer.

And, on his way to earth, Caleb often stops at the moon for a very special purpose. He kicks up some moon dust and lets it float into orbit.

If you are outside some clear night you might see a hazy ring around a full, bright moon. Caleb has been at work. He's leaving this message: "When you act in love, you might be the answer to someone's prayers."

Caleb's Assignment

Caleb loved his work as heaven's only angel-at-large. But he realized that his newest assignment was a tough one.

You might think that Caleb was worried. But angels don't worry. They realize that God can do all things. They trust God completely.

Yet, Caleb was young and very new to this work. So he didn't have much experience yet. He did trust God, but he also almost worried. (Although angels don't actually worry, they do come close to worrying sometimes. Then they say that they are almost worried.) Caleb wondered if he could really handle this assignment.

"You are to bring a message to Paul," Stephanie had told him. Stephanie was a mature angel who often brought Caleb his assignments.

"You mean the apostle Paul?" Caleb had asked in surprise. He could hardly believe his ears. He knew that Paul was very special to Jesus.

"Yes, the apostle Paul," Stephanie had answered calmly. "And then you must watch him closely for a while. His guardian angel may need some help."

That last sentence concerned Caleb. You see, Caleb knew that Paul was an extra bold mortal. (Angels always call people who live on earth mortals.) Paul stopped at nothing to tell others about Jesus. Because of that, Satan was very jealous, and he constantly tried to get at Paul.

Guardian angels are well aware of Satan. Part of their work is to keep him from stealing mortals from God. But guardian angels are bold angels. And Caleb was rather timid.

"I sure hope that I can handle this assignment," Caleb mumbled nervously.

He had found himself a soft cloud and had settled there to watch Paul.

"Of course you can, Caleb," a deep voice said behind him. "I'm Marcus, Paul's guardian angel. Let me tell you a bit about the situation." He came up next to Caleb on the cloud. "See that boat sailing in the ocean?" he asked. Caleb squinted, then nodded. "Paul is sailing toward Rome in that boat. He's supposed to appear before the Roman emperor. But Satan will try anything to stop Paul. That's why we must remain extra alert.

"God has also already said that Paul will make it to Rome, so we know that's a sure thing. Yet I must help him on his way. You're supposed to help me because Satan is giving this one his best shot. Satan is one frustrated, fallen angel. And he's very, very crafty. He'll do anything to snatch one of God's children from him.

"Mortals don't always understand Satan's power. And they don't often understand how God works. But the bottom line is that God is stronger than Satan and he will not let one of his children fall forever into Satan's hands. So, you're on the winning side, Caleb." Marcus reached over to pat Caleb's head.

"Just keep your eye on things," he finished. "Soon the ship will hit stormy weather. That's when you're supposed to give your message to Paul." Marcus then disappeared from the cloud.

So Caleb kept a close watch on earth. He didn't even go back to his heavenly mansion. And he gave no thought to wandering the streets of gold. He stayed right out there on a cloud or in a field where he could see clearly.

That's how he knew that Paul's ship was in trouble almost before Paul did. Caleb sat next to the bubbling brook where God keeps the rain before sending it back to earth. Immediately he noticed that the brook was very, very low. "It's almost out of water," he thought to himself. "Uh-oh, there's a big storm somewhere on earth."

Caleb shot over to the clouds where lightning bolts are stacked when they're not in use. "More than the usual amount are missing," he gasped. "This must be a monster storm."

As he flew to the lowest cloud he could find he heard the storm. A mighty CRACK split the air as a lightning bolt hurtled to earth. A deafening thunder roll followed. Water gushed from the brook. Caleb peered over the edge of the cloud. Paul's ship rolled helplessly in the sea. The storm raged around it.

"This is it," Caleb thought. "I'm as ready as I'll ever be," he prayed silently. "Just tell me when and where to go and what to say."

"Now!" Stephanie appeared at his side and yelled over the thunder. "God will give you the words. Go to Paul in the ship. Follow his prayer beam."

Caleb concentrated on the ship, looking for Paul's prayer beam. (Any angel who concentrates can see mortal prayers. They look like laser beams shooting up toward heaven.) But Caleb saw only confusion below. Prayer beams shot out in all directions.

"Paul's with mortals who worship other gods," Stephanie appeared and hastily explained. "That's why those beams are shooting sideways to nowhere. Look for the strong one that's coming straight up to heaven. There it is!" She pointed and gave Caleb a little shove toward earth.

The ship jolted as Caleb thudded onto it. But no one noticed; it had been rocking and reeling in the storm anyway. Immediately, he flew through the walls to Paul's cabin.

"You've come," Marcus greeted him. "I'm glad you're here to give your message. I'm busy enough right now, just keeping him alive." Just then a lantern came flying through the air straight at Paul's head. Marcus reached out and directed it to the floor.

"Look at Paul. He isn't even worried! And he can't even see me. But he is looking at you, Caleb. Do you know your message?"

"Of course," Caleb whispered. "Do not be afraid, Paul," he spoke loudly and clearly. "You must stand trial before Caesar; and God has graciously given you the lives of all who sail with you."

"Thank you, Lord," Paul murmured in response. That was it.

"You may go." Marcus glanced at Caleb. "I've got this under control. But keep us in your sight. God said that he was going to use you here again."

So Caleb shot upward through the ship to a low storm cloud. He held on tightly as it churned through the sky. But he managed to peer over the edge and find the ship tossing on the sea.

On earth, several days passed as the storm raged on. Caleb stayed gripped to his cloud. He watched in amazement as Marcus calmly turned the ship away from dangerous rocks. He saw Marcus stop sailors who were going to abandon the ship. Best of all, he watched the guardian angel save Paul from sailors who plotted to kill him.

"Marcus is so wise and so bold," Caleb thought to himself. "He recognizes all of Satan's schemes and knows exactly what to do. And he doesn't hesitate one bit."

"Oh, God," he prayed silently, "help me to do this right. Tell me what to do and when to do it." Then he turned his attention back to earth.

The storm had calmed somewhat, but Caleb's cloud still dripped rain. It was quite dark down there. "Oops, where are they?" he wondered aloud.

"Right there, Caleb!" Sophie, Caleb's very good angel friend, landed next to him with a thump. "I've been watching too. They're all off the ship and on that little island. See, they're building a fire on the beach."

"I see it now," Caleb answered her.

Suddenly, something looked strange to Caleb. "Who's that large shiny being down there?" he asked.

"Oh, my goodness," Sophie gasped. "That's Satan himself. Mortals can't see him, but Marcus can. What's going on? Satan is trying to get Marcus's attention away from Paul."

"Of course!" Caleb shouted. "Look at that snake! It's slithering straight toward Paul. It's not acting normal at all. It has no fear of mortals."

"Look sharp, Caleb," Sophie said in a rush. "This may be it. Satan probably messed with that snake so that it will bite Paul."

"That won't happen!" Caleb yelled. "Get out of there!" And with a mighty rush he punched his way right through the storm cloud in an effort to reach earth.

For one brief, shining moment, all eyes around the fire turned upward toward that cloud. Heavenly sunlight flooded through the hole that Caleb had made.

"Look at that sunbeam!" a sailor shouted. "The storm's over."

"But the fight isn't over yet," thought Caleb. "Look at the snake," he whispered urgently to Paul. But he whispered a little too urgently. Everyone around the bonfire felt it. They all stared in horror at the snake as it fastened itself to Paul's hand.

Now, the next part happened in much less time than it takes to tell. Everything took place in the blink of an eye.

"What should I do?" Caleb wondered urgently. Then he had an idea. "If Satan can stop that snake from being afraid of mortals, I can stop its venom. I'll stick my hand right into its mouth and stop up all that poison."

But Caleb had never dealt with snakes. He hesitated just a bit. He didn't know exactly where to put his hand.

Suddenly Caleb felt his hand move. It felt like a big, strong hand took his, guided it into the snake's mouth, and gently pushed his fingers into just the right places. Caleb's fingers plugged up all the poison! Not a bit of poison went into Paul!

As this was happening, a beam of light fell on Caleb's face. He looked up toward the hole he had punched into the cloud. He was just in time to see Jesus looking down at him. As he looked, Jesus slowly drew his hand up through the hole.

At the same time, Paul felt the snake bite him. He shook his hand and the snake fell into the fire.

Marcus heard the people gasp. He turned around just in time to see the snake fall. When he turned back, Satan had disappeared in defeat.

With a large smile, Marcus returned to Caleb, who stood protectively over Paul. "That was it, Caleb," he whispered. "You were wonderful. Thank you."

"It wasn't me," Caleb protested.

"God used you," Marcus replied. "I think it's time for you to rest. Look at you; you're shaking."

And so he was. Caleb had never felt the hand of God so strongly before that. With a grateful sigh he slowly winged his way toward heaven.

As he came up through the hole he had punched, he noticed first that the cloud had become white and fluffy. The storm was finally over. Then he saw the multitudes of heavenly hosts gathered on the cloud, waiting for him.

"Well done, Caleb!" they cheered.

"What a wonderful angel-at-large," some said.

"How did you know what to do?" a newer angel asked.

Behind the heavenly hosts, Jesus himself smiled with love at Caleb. The little angel-at-large scurried through the angel crowd and fell at Jesus' feet. "Thank you. Thank you, Jesus," he murmured. "I was in your hands."

Caleb hasn't been worried about any assignment since then. He doesn't always understand God's plans, but he does know that God can do all things. And he trusts God completely. Sometimes, he even tries to help mortals trust God.

At times when the storms are especially threatening, look toward the heavens. You may see a beam of sunshine shoot through a hole in one dark cloud. That's Caleb reminding you that you are in God's hands.

Caleb's Vision

Caleb hadn't played his trumpet for quite some time. He had been busy bringing messages from heaven to earth. Because he felt just a bit rusty, he took his trumpet to a cloud at the edge of heaven to practice.

He hadn't played more than one "Hallelujah" when he heard another angel land behind him. He quickly put his trumpet down, turned around, and saw Stephanie.

"I thought I'd find you here." She smiled at Caleb. "I've got an assignment for you from Jesus. He will explain all of the details later, but he wants you to start thinking about it now. Jesus says that you're supposed to show a very important vision to a mortal near Israel." (Angels always call people who live on earth mortals.)

"Show a vision?" Caleb's eyes grew big, and he almost dropped his trumpet. "I've never done visions."

"Jesus knows that," Stephanie assured him. "That's why he's sending Zach to meet you. Zach's done visions about as long as mortals have been on earth. He'll give you some helpful hints." And Stephanie disappeared.

Caleb quickly tucked his trumpet under a thick bit of cloud fluff. He had barely turned to scan the heavens when Zach appeared at his side.

"Sometime soon, I'd like you to help me with the trumpet," he said without introduction. "I've heard you play with the angel choir; you're terrific. Will you give me some pointers, Caleb?"

Caleb merely nodded his head. He always felt tongue-tied in front of angels like Zach, who had been in heaven almost forever. They weren't exactly

102

older than Caleb, because angels don't grow old. But they had *so* much more experience.

"That's why I'm here," Zach said, reading Caleb's thoughts. "I understand that this is your first vision and that it's a very important one. I'll help you any way I can. Have you done any dreams?"

Yes, Caleb said he had done a few dreams. But they were small, only a few little insights.

"Then you know that dreams are within mortals' heads," Zach went on. "Visions are different. They're real. Mortals honestly see them. And we help make visions happen.

"Jesus will tell you what to put into the vision. And, if Jesus says that the vision should be written, tell the mortal to write it down. Then make sure that the vision is written down just as you brought it."

"Why?" Caleb wondered aloud.

"Mortals have imperfect memories," Zach sighed. "They even forget things that God tells them. They need to be reminded again and again.

"Besides that, usually only one mortal sees a vision. Sometimes God wants other mortals to know that vision too.

"Is there anything else you must know right now?" Zach paused while Caleb shook his head. "Good! How about a little trumpet duet?" He pulled a fine golden trumpet from one of his sleeves. "I took this along when I was told to see you." And the two angels played several fine "Hallelujahs" before Zach left.

Now, you must remember that Caleb was a rather shy angel. He didn't quite dare discuss with Zach everything that was on his mind. So, as soon as he was alone again, he went to Sophie, his very best angel friend. He found her perched

high atop a rainbow that stretched between clouds.

"Sophie, Sophie," he whispered as he landed, ever so gently, next to her. "I have to show a vision, and I may have to be sure it's written. I don't understand about mortal books. Zach told me some; but can you help me understand a little better?"

"I was just watching a mortal write," Sophie smiled. "Just look down there into Rome. You remember Paul, don't you? Well, he's writing a letter right now. God's Spirit is helping him."

"You mean that God helps mortals when they write?" Caleb asked.

"Not all the time," Sophie answered. "Mortals often write things that they think up in their heads. There are lots of scrolls and books down there. Some are good; some aren't. That's not so important.

"But God is helping them write a very special book. It's all about how he loves mortals and what he promises them.

"This rainbow was a sign to help mortals remember something God said. But they forgot that right away. Now a rainbow is just a pretty sight to them. So much for signs.

"God wants certain things that he says to mortals written down perfectly for them. That's to be God's special book. It has taken a long time, but it's almost finished. Zach can tell you about some of the first visions he gave for that book. I think that your vision is connected with God's special book too."

Caleb almost broke out into a sweat when he heard that. His forehead creased up into lots of tiny wrinkles. How could he possibly bring such an important vision? He just didn't have enough experience to be trusted with that. He turned to Sophie with such an almost-worried look that she couldn't help chuckling.

"Oh, Caleb," she sighed as she wrapped her wing around him. "You are so sweet and so humble. But you're also almost worried. I think you ought to talk to Jesus about it."

"That's exactly what Jesus wants," a voice broke in. Stephanie looked up at them. "Why don't both of you slide down off that rainbow—carefully, please? Sophie, you are needed at the great rehearsal hall. The angel choir has a special part for you to sing. And Caleb, Jesus is calling you."

Caleb couldn't get to Jesus fast enough. He loved to sit at Jesus' feet, or on his lap, and let love flow over him. Jesus always made him feel so special. Caleb would do anything he could for Jesus. Often, after he was with Jesus, he felt like he *could* do anything.

That's what happened this time too. Jesus gave Caleb all the vision details. They were very complicated. There were to be many seals, bowls, trumpets, angels, and all sorts of action. At first, Caleb wasn't at all sure he could keep it all straight. But he listened very carefully. And, of course, he didn't forget a thing. Angels have perfect memories. But, best of all, just before Caleb left, Jesus gave him a gentle hug and said, "I'll help you, precious Caleb. I promise."

"What's a promise?" Caleb asked Zach the next time they practiced together. He was getting to know Zach a little better, so he was not quite as shy as he had been earlier.

"Oh, that's a mortal word," Zach said and grinned at his friend. "Sometimes mortals say that they'll do things and then forget to do them. A promise is a stronger way of saying that they *will* do

something. Jesus always does what he says. He used that word so that you would be sure he will help you. Someday, you may have to use it with mortals. Now, can we play that summons tune again?" (A summons tune is one used to call many angels together.)

"I really should work on that vision," Caleb answered. "I've got to talk to lots of angels and get lots of things together yet."

"You won't make a mistake," Zach assured him. "I felt just like you the first time I brought a vision. You probably have a small case of nerves. But Jesus always makes sure that it goes perfectly. He's promised. And I'll help you get things ready if you help me practice that summons tune."

So Zach and Caleb played their trumpets for quite some time. And they practiced together quite often. In fact, they became very good friends because they had so much in common.

Caleb loved to play duets with another angel who felt as rusty at trumpet as he did. Actually, they were both very good. They often laughed in sheer joy, or surprise, at the music they made.

Zach loved to tell Caleb about visions and messages he had brought when mortals were new to earth. And Caleb listened eagerly, because they were stories about things before his time. Sometimes they even laughed at Zach's stories. Not at the mortals, mind you, or at the messages; just at the stories. Zach was a very good storyteller.

"And so, I finally had to make this donkey talk," Zach was saying one time. "I don't think an earthly donkey ever talked before then. And I think the donkey was more surprised than—"

"I'm sorry to interrupt, but it's time for the vision." Of course, it was Stephanie. "Caleb, Jesus wants you to gather the

trumpets, bowls, and other things, then summon the angels who will assist you. Take them to a man called John on the island called Patmos. See the rainbow over that island there? Just follow it to its western end. You'll find John there."

"I'll help," Zach volunteered. So the two angels gathered everything that Caleb needed.

"Let's summon the angels ourselves," Zach suggested. So they played a summons tune and all the angels that Caleb needed came quickly.

Caleb led the procession to earth. They were all invisible, as planned, of course. But Caleb knew he must do something to catch John's attention. And so, as they followed the rainbow, Caleb added one more bow on top of it.

Most mortals had forgotten the true message of a rainbow, just as Sophie had said. But John had not forgotten. He had read about it in God's special book. And no mortal had seen a double rainbow before this time. So when John saw the double rainbow, he paid attention right away.

The vision began to unfold exactly as Jesus had said. Caleb told each angel what to do when. He made sure that each bowl and seal and anything else came and went when it was supposed to. He was especially careful with the trumpets.

That's why Caleb looked around in surprise when he called for an angel trumpeter, and no one came forward. Quickly he looked around at all the angels he had assembled. One was missing! What had happened? What should he do?

Then Zach stepped forward. "I'll do it," he said. So Zach stepped in and did exactly what he was supposed to do.

The rest of the vision went perfectly. Caleb remembered to tell John to write it all down. And he assured John that all the words were trustworthy and true. Of course, Jesus was there, just as he had promised. But Caleb didn't hear Jesus until . . .

"I, Jesus, have sent my angel to give you this testimony," Caleb heard Jesus say to John. And the little angel looked up just in time to see Jesus smile gently at him.

"Jesus helped me throughout the vision, just as he promised he would," Caleb whispered to Zach. And then the vision was finished.

Many days later, Caleb and Zach sat on a cloud close to earth watching John write. Caleb was determined to stay right there until John had written every word correctly.

"Zach," Caleb wondered aloud. "Did Jesus tell you to follow me?"

"Yes," his friend answered. "Jesus knows that sometimes angels are called away from a vision at the very last minute. Usually, the angel who is in charge takes a few extras along. So Jesus told me to go along as a substitute. That was a little extra help he gave you—"

"Hey, Zach, is that description of heaven right?" interrupted Caleb. "John's words don't make it sound as beautiful as it really is."

"That's because mortal words can't describe heaven's beauty," Zach answered. "Look at what he's writing at the end. He's warning all mortals to add

120

nothing to the book. Do you know what, Caleb? That's the very last part of God's special book. You brought the very last vision for the book!"

"I'm glad I didn't know that before I went." Caleb heaved a sigh of relief. "I would have been more almost-worried.

"Yet," he added, "I knew that I could trust Jesus. He always keeps his promises. But, I don't have to tell *you* that."

Even today Caleb thinks that mortals need to be reminded. So, once in a while, he searches until he finds a rainbow already in the sky. Then, very carefully, he adds another set of colors to make it a double rainbow. That's his way of saying to mortals, "Jesus always keeps his promises."